Santa's Snow Cat

By Sue Stainton

Illustrated by Anne Mortimer

HARPERCOLLINSPUBLISHERS

To Alex, Sam, and Charlie
—S.S.

To Andrew, Linda, and George
and a special thank-you
to Penny and her beautiful snow cat
—A.M.

Santa's Snow Cat

SANTA'S favorite cat was the color of snow. She
would hide in the snowdrifts and be invisible to the
world. Even the North Wind and the big Lemon
Moon, who lit up the winter sky, never guessed she was
there, and they knew almost everything.

She would hide in Santa's beard, nestle up, and keep
warm during the cold Arctic nights. She would snuggle and
purr deep in his coat pockets, and stow away on
mysterious journeys.

It was her secret.

SANTA called her Snow Cat, but this whitest of cats had the greenest of eyes, and in the moonlight her eyes would gleam the color of jade. That was just how the North Wind found out about his new playmate.

IT was the coldest of winter nights. The North Wind had blown snow into a kaleidoscope of patterns and decked the land with necklaces of icicles, which the big Lemon Moon turned into diamonds.

The North Wind was bored, but suddenly he heard a swish in the snow and saw two jewel green eyes shining in the light of the Lemon Moon. He spiraled gently and whooshed with delight.

Snow Cat danced.

Together they whirled and they twirled, and the Lemon Moon watched and lit up the night.

IT was the night before Christmas, and the Lemon Moon knew that it was time for a magical journey, so he lit the way for Snow Cat to go home. The North Wind huffed just a little and watched as she went into the icy, snowy house.

Secretly Snow Cat found the red snuggly, cuddly coat and crawled into a big, warm, furry pocket. Santa laughed a great happy laugh as he flung on his coat. "It's the night before Christmas!" Santa shouted.

In a jingle of bells and a flurry of snow they swished into the air.

Santa reached into his pocket for a mitten and found his Snow Cat. He pretended to be annoyed, but then he laughed.

IN a magical moment, Snow Cat balanced on Santa's fat red knee as she looked down on a white carpet of frosted ice sculptures sparkling in the moonlight, spattered with twinkling, winking lights. In a second she was up so high, looking down at frozen seas, studded with great icebergs the size of cathedrals.

The Lemon Moon lit the way.

The North Wind swirled around.

It all took Snow Cat's breath away.

A MOMENT later, a mass of colored lights spiraled in a maze beneath her. Snow Cat shook her freezing whiskers and excitedly looked a little closer at the pattern of lights far below. She was enchanted. She twitched her nose and wondered what life was like down there—but then leaned too far. She fell.

Santa's big mittens tried to catch her. The North Wind tried to cushion her. The Lemon Moon closed his eyes. But Snow Cat still fell—tumbling, twisting, and turning toward the lights below. The North Wind carried Santa's words down to her: "Snow Cat, Snow Cat, my favorite cat, I will find you!"

SNOW Cat wondered where she had landed. There were strange noises, flashing, brightly colored lights, new smells, people chattering, traffic clanking, and hustle and bustle everywhere.

She wanted to hide.

She had heard the cry and knew that Santa would be looking for her. My Santa, I must find you, she thought.

Snow Cat trudged gingerly up the white street. Nimbly she dodged people's feet—so many people. So many shoes, so many different types of shoes. Some people spoke. "Hey, pussycat," they said, but like quicksilver she avoided them.

NOW Snow Cat looked up, and towering above her were huge, tall buildings embossed with yellow lights that reached forever toward the starry, inky sky. Large snowflakes fell all around, but she couldn't see the Lemon Moon or hear the North Wind.

SUDDENLY she raced ahead to find herself nose-to-nose with Santa. Something was wrong. A nearly Santa, cold and bright, swinging slightly, beckoned her to a brightly lit store. Windows full of shimmering gold and silver swam before her eyes.

It wasn't her Santa. Despondently she moved on. Her paws were cold, her whiskers frozen.

ECHOING Christmas carols reached the confused
ears of Snow Cat. She heard singing and calling, but
when she looked up her eyes were glazed with flashing
colors. She focused on a Santa all made of bright lights who
was singing "Ho! Ho! Ho!"

It wasn't her Santa. Now it was snowing thickly. And
where was the North Wind? The Lemon Moon was hiding,
and it seemed that even the stars were asleep.

Surely her Santa could not be far away.

AHEAD, laughing a large, jolly laugh in the shadow of a tall sparkling tree, was the red figure at last! She hurtled toward him and jumped onto the well-loved knee. But the knee was bony, the voice angry, and this was not her Santa!

She jumped down, tumbling piles of parcels and trailing tinsel, and ran from the nearly Santa.

Surely her Santa could not be far away.

THE night grew still as she waded through the new snow. People were busily disappearing into doorways. Snow Cat was desperate. Then, as she passed an old wooden door decorated with mistletoe and holly berries, she heard a familiar "Ho! Ho! Ho!" and wearily she squeezed in through a chink in the doorway.

THE house was warm and she followed the noise.
Notes of festive music wafted in the air, and the scent
of pine needles and oranges was everywhere.

As Snow Cat turned a corner, she had another shock.
A smiling Santa was looking out from the flickering screen—
another nearly Santa!

FRIGHTENED, she turned quickly and gently knocked the glittering tree. It twinkled, just as though it were laughing at her.

Snow Cat looked up, and a glass ball fell between her paws. She looked again, and saw that the glass ball was yet another nearly Santa, shining and smiling at her.

Snow Cat sank to the ground. She had given up. She slept with the littlest Santa between her paws.

It was not until much, much later that she awoke. She was now sure that her Santa had forgotten her.

IF only Snow Cat had known that Santa and his sleigh
had spiraled down wildly after her and had landed on
the tallest of tall buildings.

Santa was still searching, along with the North Wind
and the big Lemon Moon.

S NOW Cat awoke in the nighttime glint of the
Christmas lights. The house was so quiet, so still.
Her ears twitched and picked up a sound far away,
then her whiskers twitched, then her nose twitched. A moment
later—to a sound of clumping and guffawing—she was
looking at big, black, snowy boots and up at a fat, snuggly,
cuddly coat. And was that her big, warm, furry pocket?

Could it be Santa?

"Snow Cat! My best Christmas present," Santa whispered.
He scooped her up and laughed his great jolly laugh.

THAT night the North Wind blew a homeward path in the falling snow for Santa and his favorite cat. Since that Christmas, Santa always travels with his Snow Cat, and sometimes, even now, they are glimpsed on the tallest of tall buildings.

Santa's Snow Cat

Text copyright © 2001 by Sue Stainton

Illustrations copyright © 2001 by Anne Mortimer

Printed in the U.S.A. All rights reserved.

www.harperchildrens.com

Library of Congress Cataloging-in-Publication Data

Stainton, Sue.

Santa's Snow Cat / by Sue Stainton ; illustrations by Anne Mortimer.—

1st ed.

p.   cm.

Summary: Santa and his favorite cat search for each other after she falls

out of his sleigh and lands in New York City on Christmas Eve.

ISBN 0-06-623827-7 — ISBN 0-06-623828-5 (lib. bdg.)

[1. Cats—Fiction. 2. Santa Claus—Fiction. 3. Christmas—Fiction.

4. Lost and found possessions—Fiction. 5. New York (N.Y.)—Fiction.]

I. Mortimer, Anne, ill. II. Title.

PZ7.S782555 San 2001

[E]—dc21   2001024163

Typography by Al Cetta

1 2 3 4 5 6 7 8 9 10

First Edition